U0902258

Anne of Green Gables

绿山墙的安妮

【加】蒙哥马利◎著　麦芒◎译

天津出版传媒集团
天津人民出版社

图书在版编目（CIP）数据

绿山墙的安妮 / (加) 蒙哥马利著 ; 麦芒译. -- 天津 : 天津人民出版社，2016.5
ISBN 978-7-201-10248-1

Ⅰ. ①绿… Ⅱ. ①蒙… ②麦… Ⅲ. ①儿童文学—长篇小说—加拿大—现代 Ⅳ. ①I711.84

中国版本图书馆CIP数据核字（2016）第073543号

绿山墙的安妮
LV SHAN QIANG DE AN NI

出　　版　天津人民出版社
出 版 人　黄　沛
地　　址　天津市和平区西康路35号康岳大厦
邮政编码　300051
邮购电话　（022）23332469
网　　址　http: //www.tjrmcbs.com
电子信箱　tjrmcbs@126.com
责任编辑　刘子伯
印　　刷　北京欣睿虹彩印刷有限公司
经　　销　新华书店
开　　本　880×1230毫米　1/32
印　　张　8.5
插　　页　8
字　　数　260千字
版次印次　2016年5月第1版　2016年5月第1次印刷
定　　价　26.80元

Anne knelt in front of Marilla's knees, looking up at her solemnly. (P45)

The small valley with flowers everywhere was surrounded by alders, a brook meandering through. (P1)

The Moon and Sixpence

月亮和六便士

[英] 毛 姆◎著 麦 芒◎译

天津出版传媒集团
天津人民出版社

图书在版编目（CIP）数据

月亮和六便士 / (英) 毛姆著 ; 麦芒译. -- 天津 :
天津人民出版社，2017.2 (2019.1重印)
ISBN 978-7-201-11445-3

Ⅰ. ①月… Ⅱ. ①毛… ②麦… Ⅲ. ①长篇小说—英
国—现代 Ⅳ. ①I561.45

中国版本图书馆CIP数据核字（2017）第034862号

月亮和六便士

YUE LIANG HE LIU BIAN SHI

出　　版　天津人民出版社
出 版 人　刘　庆
地　　址　天津市和平区西康路35号康岳大厦
邮政编码　300051
邮购电话　（022）23332469
网　　址　http: //www.tjrmcbs.com
电子信箱　tjrmcbs@126.com
责任编辑　王昊静
印　　刷　北京智慧源印刷有限公司
经　　销　新华书店
开　　本　880×1230毫米　1/32
印　　张　10
插　　页　6
字　　数　320千字
版次印次　2017年2月第1版　2019年5月第3次印刷
定　　价　32.80元

Mrs. Strickland, 37 years old, was slightly taller and plump, but not too fat.
(P19)

Strickland was not too handsome, but a little taller than I thought. (P27)

I have to draw. (P62)

Strickland was engrossed in the chess game in front of him.
(P100)

The house is half made of housing and half of the studio.

(P122)

It must have been a strange feeling that Bronshettev had been with the patient night and day. (P154)